Peter Rabbit™

LILY'S PARTY TIME

PUFFIN

Map of my woods

This is a map of the woods where I live. You can see who else lives here too. It's in my dad's journal which I always have with me.

ROCKY ISLAND

Jeremy Fisher loves making music. (But he's not very good at it!)

OLD BROWN'S ISLAND

MR JEREMY FISHER'S POND

SQUIRREL NUTKIN'S WOOD

MRS TIGGY-WINKLE'S LAUNDRY

Sneaky **Samuel Whiskers** is a notorious cake thief.

This is **Mr Tod**. Foxes eat rabbits. Need I say more?

JEMIMA PUDDLE-DUCK'S
HILLTOP FARM

MR MCGREGOR'S
GARDEN

MR TOD & TOMMY
BROCK'S WOOD

MY BURROW

DR & MRS BOBTAIL'S
BURROW (LILY'S HOME)

TUNNEL
NETWORK

MR BOUNCER'S BURROW
(BENJAMIN'S HOME)

RAVINE

DEEP DARK WOODS

DANDELION FIELD

My friend,
Lily Bobtail.
Whatever the
problem, she's
got the answer.

Benjamin Bunny is
my cousin. Whatever
I do, he's right behind
me – usually hiding!

It was a sunny summer's day, and beside
the lake everyone was looking forward to
Jeremy Fisher's concert party.

Everyone, that was,
except Peter Rabbit.

"I'd rather be having an adventure," muttered Peter.

"But there's going to be a big party afterwards," said Lily. "It'll be so much fun!"

"Mmm, look at the cakes!" said Benjamin.

The cake table looked amazing, but Peter still felt grumpy.

"Welcome to my concert," announced Jeremy Fisher. And he began to play . . . **VERY** badly!

Feeling bored, Peter gazed around at the reeds . . . and spied Samuel Whiskers sneaking up to steal the party cakes!

"We have to stop him!"
Peter whispered to Lily and Benjamin.

The three friends quickly hopped over to the cake table.

"You can't eat those cakes," said Lily.
"They're for the party."

"You can't stop me!"
Samuel Whiskers replied rudely.

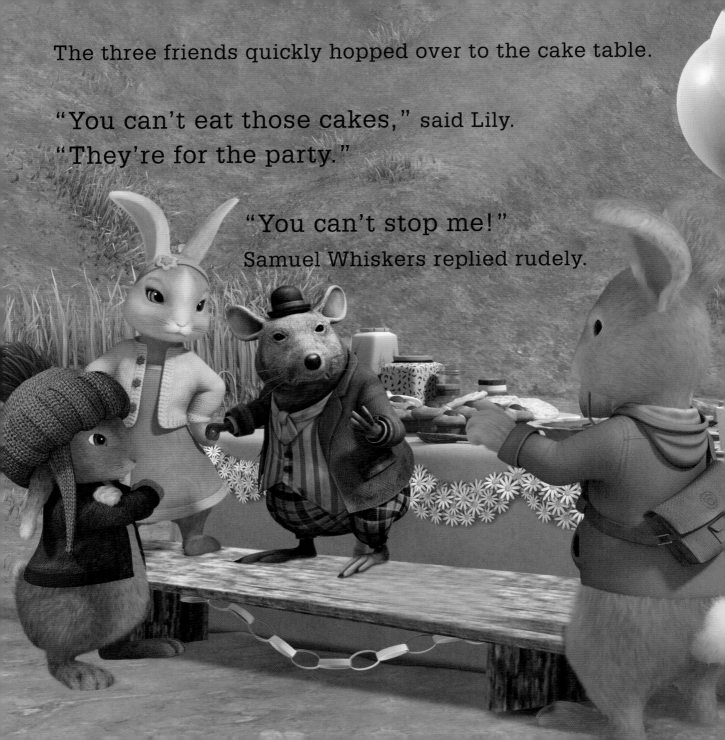

"Just watch us!"
said Peter.

Together, the bunnies lifted one end of
the bench, and the rat slid to the ground.

BUMP!

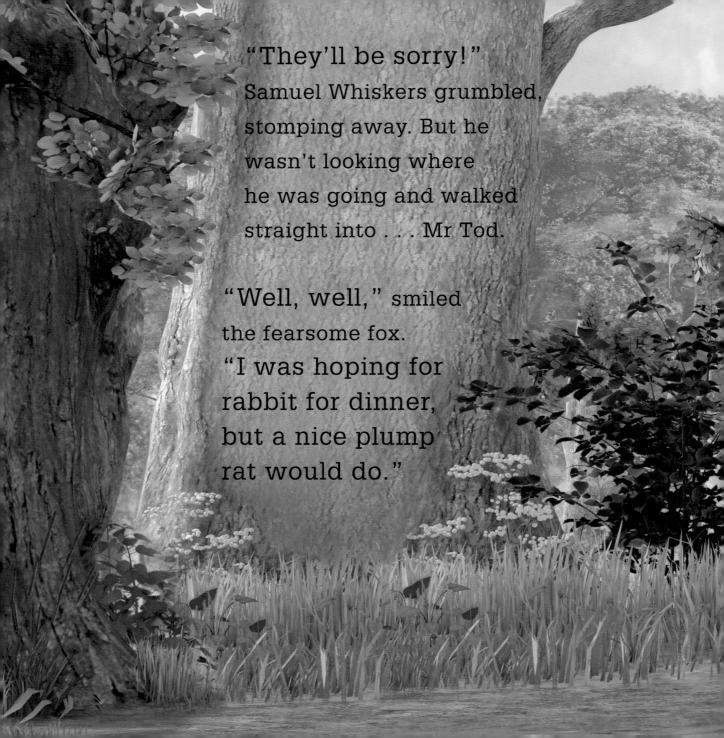

"They'll be sorry!"
Samuel Whiskers grumbled,
stomping away. But he
wasn't looking where
he was going and walked
straight into . . . Mr Tod.

"Well, well," smiled
the fearsome fox.
"I was hoping for
rabbit for dinner,
but a nice plump
rat would do."

"D-d-don't eat me!" stammered Samuel Whiskers. "I know where you can find LOTS of rabbits."

The two villains made their way to the lake. When Mr Tod saw the audience at the concert, he chuckled.

"Well done, Mr Whiskers," he said. "Rabbits for me and cake for you. A feast!"

But sharp-eyed Lily spied his
bushy tail among the reeds.

"It's Mr Tod!"
she yelled.
"RUN!"

Everyone raced towards the woods with
Mr Tod chasing after them.

Samuel Whiskers grabbed a yummy muffin.
"Ha ha, this is the funniest thing
I've seen in ages," he giggled.

"We've got to do
something!"

said Lily.

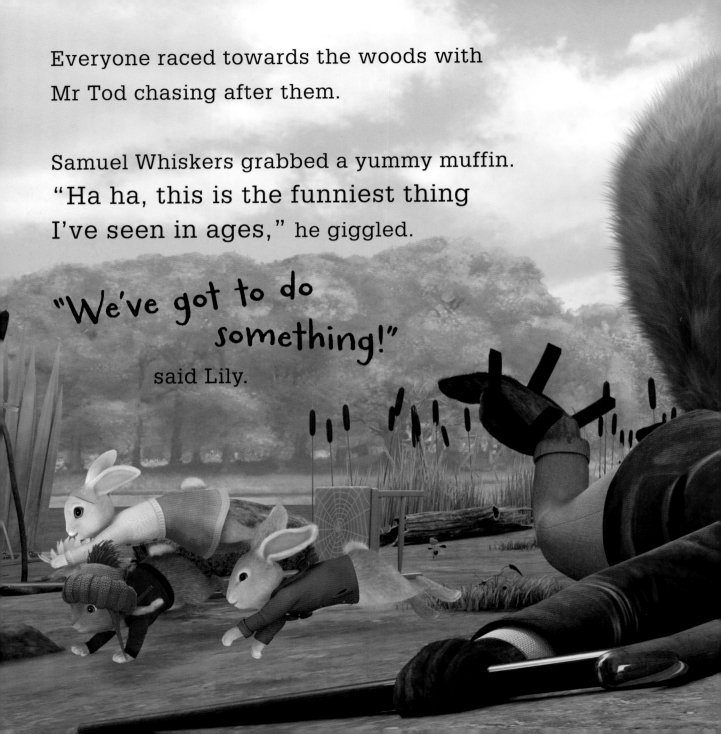

Thinking fast, Peter grabbed
a stool and threw it under
Mr Tod's feet.

CRASH!

The fox fell head over heels, and
the rabbits dashed past him.

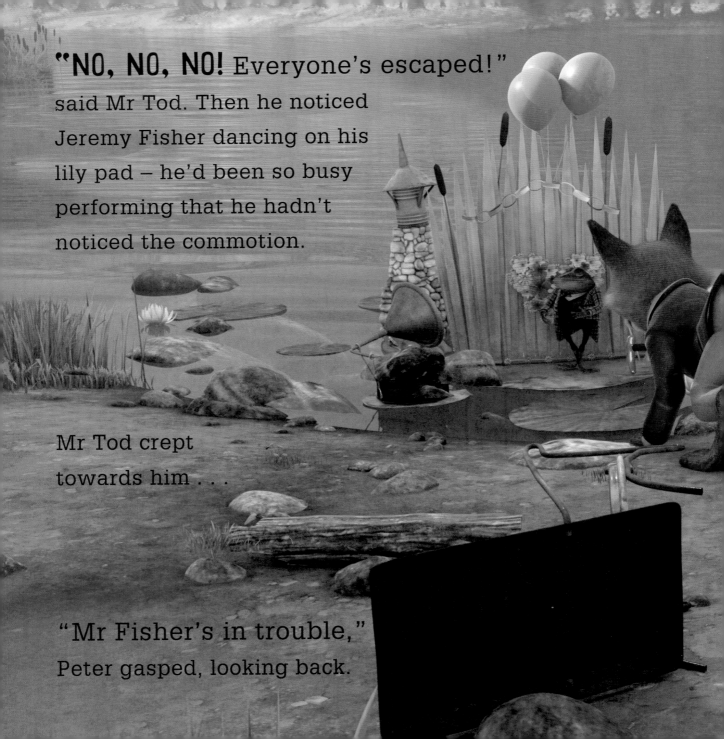

"**NO, NO, NO!** Everyone's escaped!"
said Mr Tod. Then he noticed
Jeremy Fisher dancing on his
lily pad – he'd been so busy
performing that he hadn't
noticed the commotion.

Mr Tod crept
towards him . . .

"Mr Fisher's in trouble,"
Peter gasped, looking back.

"Hungry foxes eat frogs," said Lily.
"I know that for a fact."

"We have to save him!"

Peter, Lily and Benjamin
raced back to the lake.

Mr Tod was opening
his mouth wide, ready
to pounce . . .

"NO!"

yelled Peter.

He pushed Jeremy Fisher out of harm's
way – just in time! Then he shoved a
violin bow into Mr Tod's open jaws.

SNAP!  Mr Tod bit the bow in two.

"Grrr, I'll get you, Peter Rabbit!"
he said.

"A good rabbit never gives up!" cried Peter.
He turned to Benjamin and Lily. "Let's make
some music of our own!"

"Let's do it!"
cheered Lily.

"Rabbits are brave. Rabbits
are brave," said Benjamin.

DONK!

As Mr Tod pounced, Lily used Jeremy Fisher's violin as a shield.

TWANG!

Peter loudly strummed a banjo string in Mr Tod's ear.

BASH! Benjamin drummed a tune on the startled fox's head.

Mr Tod tumbled into the lake with a huge **SPLASH!**

"We did it!" cried Peter.

Mr Tod crawled out of the lake and squelched away, and Samuel Whiskers scurried off into the woods.

"Can we eat the cakes now?" Benjamin asked hopefully.

"Let's hop to it!" replied Peter.

As all the bunnies' family and friends came back, cheering and clapping, Jeremy Fisher started singing a merry tune.

"Let's dance!" said Lily.

"It's party time!"

JEREMY FISHER'S MUSICAL MOMENTS

Mr Fisher has lots of musical instruments. Each one makes very different music, but they ALL sound much better than his terrible singing! Here's a sketch from my dad's journal.

Violin and bow – screeeech! (Cover your ears!)

Trumpet – toot! Toot!

Hold Your Own CONCERT PARTY

Peter didn't want to go to Jeremy Fisher's concert, but making music can be fun!

YOU CAN MAKE YOUR OWN INSTRUMENTS:

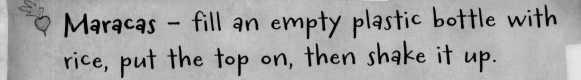

- **Maracas** – fill an empty plastic bottle with rice, put the top on, then shake it up.

- **Cymbals** – clang two saucepan lids together.

- **Drums** – bash upturned saucepans with wooden spoons.

- **Banjo** – stretch elastic bands over an empty tissue box or cake tin – twang!

Why not put on a concert for your family and friends?

CONGRATULATIONS!
SKILL IN MUSIC MAKING CERTIFICATE

Awarded to

- -

- -

Age

- -

Jeremy Fisher
- - - - - - - - - - - - - - - - - -
MR JEREMY FISHER
BEST MUSICIAN IN THE WOODS
(OR SO HE THINKS . . .)

Bravo! Magnificent
music making.